ANCIENT OF DAYS

(Author Of All You Survey)

ANCIENT OF DAYS

(Author Of All You Survey)

Grover Grumpy Pitman

ARPress
ILLUMINATING IDEAS
EMPOWERING VOICES

ARPress
45 Dan Road Suite 5
Canton MA 02021

Hotline: 1(888) 821-0229
Fax: 1(508) 545-7580

Ordering Information:

Quantity sales. Special discounts are available on quantity purchases by corporations, associations, and others. For details, contact the publisher at the address above.

Printed in the United States of America.

ISBN-13:   Softcover   979-8-89389-529-2
               eBook   979-8-89389-530-8

Library of Congress Control Number: 2024920048

TABLE OF CONTENTS

INTRODUCTION

ONCE UPON A TIME

struggle, I wiggle, I claw at the rocks. Almost there, a little more, a little more. My stone confinement tumbles down around me and I am out.

My throat is parched, gritty and in immediate need of relief. I survey the area and locate a canteen a few feet away. I pick it up and shake it. It is half full. Every indication tells me that water conservation will be a priority. I take a small sip, the contents are hot but, wet and seem to soothe the sandpaper feeling in my throat.

My surroundings are barren and arid. It looks more like an archeological dig then a once thriving metropolis. The temperature is mild. There is a refreshing breeze that stirs up little dust funnels on the terrain. The tumbleweeds playfully dance and bounce as the wind pushes them to their next destination.

My environment gives all the signs of being daylight. The sky is clear without a cloud to be seen. But, for the life of me, I cannot locate the sun. It appears everything is lit up by some other cosmic light source that eludes my perception of light.

Now things get scary. There are no people. No one alive or dead. If I were prone to panic attacks, I'm guessing this would be the opportune moment?

What keeps my sanity intact is, the glimmer of hope, that if I survived Armageddon there must be others. Fact is, I don't remember a time in my life when I really lost control of my emotions. I take that back. When I was a child of ten, maybe eleven years old, I had this nightmare. I dreamed my body was covered in locusts. They were crawling in my ears, up my nose and down my throat. I woke up screaming, my body covered in sweat.

As far as the nightmare's origin? I'm going to chalk it up to a TV special I'd, probably, seen on locusts and my imagination took over.

Well, anyway, mom rushed to my room. She cradled me in her arms, rocked me and sang: Jesus loves you this I know, for the bible tells me so. Little ones to him belong, they are weak but, he is strong. I don't know if it was her gentle voice, the words or a combination of things that seemed to calm the demons in my head. Mom would remain in the room as I attempted to get back to sleep. I could not see her but, the creaking of the rocker on the hardwood floors, assured me she was there.

OK, I'll stop the violin music, but, make no promises that it won't return. The first thing I need to do is find some writing material to record the events while they are still freshly etched in my memory. It would be all I have left to hand down to posterity. That is, if there still is a posterity?

By the way, my name is Joel Braxton. At one time I was a detective. I was born in Maryland to George, a DC cop, and Rebecca Braxton.

My Dad wasn't your lovey-dovey, kissy-huggy type. He was, however, a very tolerant and kind man. Don't get me wrong, when I over stepped boundaries my ass felt the wrath of his right hand.

Saturday night in my home was designated as family night. Mom would make popcorn, while dad chose a movie. Dad was a big John Wayne fan. So, most of the movies were old westerns, and usually in black and white.

Well, I did not care much for popcorn and the movie selection totally sucked. But, that was not what the evening was about. I would not have traded one of those nights for all the drugs and alcohol making the rounds at the local park.

Dad was not a religious man, per say. He did, however, believe in a Creator by default. The thought of being spawned from a rock, a monkey or some other creature was not a viable option.

Dad attended church twice a year, on Easter and Christmas, but, that was just to make mom happy. The rest of the year it became my responsibility to escort mom. Because, as dad put it so eloquently, I was low man on the totem pole.

Unlike dad, mom was a very pious woman. "Wait, what's that shining in the sand? A can of beans, I hate beans. What I wouldn't give for a steak, a baked potato and a nice cold beer."

Where was I before I lost my train of thought?

Oh ya, mom was very active in the church. She sang in the choir during evening service, she acted as a greeter, janitor and anything else these hypocrites deemed necessary. Yes, I did not stutter. In case I wasn't clear, hypocrites, hypocrites, hypocrites.

First off, there was old man Miller, so hung over from the previous night, he could hardly hold his head up during service.

Then there was Lucy Devane, I think that was her last name, everybody knew her as loosey-Lucy, probably the biggest cock-tease in the county.

And that's not to mention the Cohens. Their marital problems were all the ammunition the church gossips needed.

If I were to buy into this religious mumbo-jumbo, which by all appearances I was over qualified, I would have had to witness a whole lot more of this, so called, Christian behavior.

Well anyway, every Sunday, rain or shine, I was dragged to church. I believe it was a parental plot to legally torture me for a couple hours as payback for childhood crimes committed during the week. After all, as a child of five, what the hell did I know of church politics. And this God person was not in the same league with Santa Claus or the Easter bunny. So, what was the point?

As a result, I was fidgety and mischievous. Mom always came armed with shut up candy and it wasn't church unless I got the occasional smack for disorderly conduct.

As I neared puberty, my focus changed to Mrs. Hendricks. She was a rather large breasted woman who usually sat in front of us. Church people are a strange breed, it seems once they locate a seat, week after week, they claim squatter's rights on that spot. Well anyway, I can't recall if Mrs. H was young, old or middle age. Her face was not my focal point. If she owned a dress that did not start right at those milky white orbs, exposing them to anyone caring to take a peek, I had never seen it. I always enjoyed the solemn moments of prayer. I could situate myself where I could get a birds-eye view of her cleavage without being detected.

Church hadn't changed over the years. Shut up candy was replaced by eye candy and mom gave me an occasional nudge to bring me back to the real world. I wonder if mom ever caught on to what I was staring at? Oh well, it no longer matters.

Mom was a firm believer in tithing. The tithe is the first ten percent of your income belongs to God. At least, that's the entity the church passed the buck to.

We were not destitute nor were we born with a silver spoon in our mouth. So, ten percent of my dad's check was a huge chunk. Especially when he felt the tithe was like most other business deals, a shit load of promises, a bunch of excuses and zero results. Mom never asked for much, so, dad caved into her wishes on this one.

By age thirty, mom developed a brain tumor to go along with her arthritis. Between treatments, remissions, hospitals, doctors, medicine and anyone else who felt they were entitled to dig into dad's wallet our finances were getting way out of hand.

Yet mom went about her chores with a smile and a song on her lips. Dad and I did not know how to make her slow down without insulting her. We came up with a good plan, we would just become less messy. Well, I was a kid and dad was; dad, so that venture failed miserably.

By age thirty-five Mom's arthritis in her ankles and knees had become acute. She now needed the assistance of a walker to ease the pain somewhat.

"Ah, there's what I'm looking for, Solomon Heber's briefcase, there has to be some writing stuff in there."

Solomon was the wisest man I had ever met. Even in times of crisis, he was the calming voice of sanity and reason.

"Let's see what we have in here. An extra pair of glasses, maps, a bible, I'll get back to that in a moment. Here we go, pencils and paper. Now to find a comfortable spot."

I wanted to know, so badly, the hold this God seemed to have on mom. A God that re-payed loyalty and obedience with pain and suffering.

Mom had always called the bible, God's word. So what better place to start than right from the horse's mouth. I struggled through the first three chapters of Genesis. I closed the book more disappointed than when I started. I could not believe my mom was that gullible. How could she buy into this crap? I mean, C-mon, talking serpents and magical fruit? The only thing separating this book from a fairy tale is the bible does not start out, ONCE UPON A TIME:

CHAPTER 1

HOLY SMOKE

A veil of sadness filled the corridors of the Vatican. Pope Thaddeus was dead. He was a beloved man who passed away peacefully in his sleep.

It was a known fact that Pope Thaddeus was an opponent of the, very popular, World Health Care Reform. For no other reason than he believed it did not have God's stamp of approval. It started many rumors that there was foul play involved in the Pope's death. But, with no autopsy all the rumors were left to conjecture.

It was early spring and I believe it was about the time the worldwide heat wave and drought started. The temperature was lingering around 95 degrees Fahrenheit in the shade. I guess a case could have been made for global warming.

Yet, it did not stop the throngs from cramming in beneath the balcony of St. Peters Basilica in hopes of getting a glimpse of the new Pope.

Adding to the heat was the length of time it was taking to select the inevitable. Human nature was kicking in and the crowd was getting uncomfortable and agitated.

I imagine more than a few people got home without their wallet or jewelry because the pick-pockets would find these conditions prime for the performance of their chosen trade.

At long last, white smoke hovered above the Vatican. An indication that a new Pope had been selected.

A Cardinal came to the balcony and announced the words, "ANNUNTIO VOBIS GAUDIUM MAGNUM: HABEMUS PAPAM." No longer would those words be spoken again at the Vatican.

The man's name was Lucas Cain. The choice was not a surprise to the masses. He was a popular man not even in the church but also in the secular world. The man had resurrected churches, built hospitals and schools. But, his fame came from his involvement in the World Health Care Reform.

The bill was intended to level the playing field in the medical and drug industries. There were some people paying next to nothing for health care and medicine and others were paying an arm and a leg. This bill was meant to rectify the situation. Everyone would pay the same low premium for better medical attention and low drug costs, not only locally but, but worldwide.

The medical field and drug industries had no problem with the bill, they were losing nothing. Payments were just spread around and they were now dealing in volume. The bonus was now the population would consider these industries, the good guys.

The network of medical professionals took off like wildfire. Many countries made plans to subsidize for the very poor. Countries that had absorbed all the medical costs of their populace found an answer that was fair and beneficial. The people of these countries were not happy but, there was no alternative. Well you can't please everyone.

The conclave had no problem with Cain's accomplishments. It was his methods that were brought into question. Cain was considered a rebel. "No that's not the word I'm looking for. What word am I searching for? Renegade, no, Radical, yes radical, that will do nicely."

It did not take Cain long to show his radical side. He chose the title Pope Hydarnes V and replaced the "Swiss Guard" with a group called "The Immortals."

Head of security was a man named Saul Linetti. He had a general dislike for people. His face was gruff and weather beaten, almost leathery. It looked like it had been chiseled out and the sculptor had forgotten to smooth the rough edges. Let's just say, you wouldn't have liked to run into him in a dark alley.

What almost made him look civilized was his wardrobe. He always dressed in a dark three- piece suit minus the tie, black patent leather shoes and all topped off with his trademark fedora.

Linetti and Father Alexander Gray had a mutual hatred for each other. Gray was the chief advisor to the Pope, for lack of a better description.

Gray was smarter than Linetti and considered Linetti incapable of intelligent conversation and on the level of a barbarian. Saul just hated Gray period. The two of them could not be in the same room, for five minutes, before words and insults would start flying. If the arguments turned to fist-a-cuffs I would have had to bet on Linetti. In Linetti's defense he wasn't getting paid for his personality or thinking capacity.

To keep them separated, Father Gray was assigned to BarTech Industries outside of London. He was put in charge of distribution replacing Sarah Wright, an American.

BarTech Industries had been an innovative leader in electronic technology. Their biggest break through had come with a project called "Goliath." It was a small chip about the size of a pin head. When the device was inserted in your right thumb, it became your identity.

I know a lot of companies have toyed with this concept. But, no one had come near Bar- Tech's success. I am not a scientist so I'll try to explain how the devise worked, as best I can.

When inserted in the thumb, it would fuse with a person's DNA, circulatory system and electrical impulses. The chip now has become who you are. The chip is to small to hold a vast amount of information so, the answer was to use a person's brain for storage. Even if someone could not remember something, the chip could find the answer. In essence the chip knew, you better than you knew, you. The old fashion paper trail was now history.

In the event that the body ceases functioning, such as in death, the device goes dormant. I see no advantage to that unless you could be resurrected from the dead. Or maybe, temporarily expired on a surgical table. Well I won't dwell on the possibilities.

The secure feature was that no one could steal your identity. Should someone make the attempt? Well the result would be catastrophic. The DNA and other bodily functions would not mesh. It would virtually fry your brain seeking information that was not there.

The device had a bonus feature. It would send subliminal messaging 24-7 showing the beauty and advantage of a one world government.

It did what it was meant to do. It disrupted a governments infrastructure, causing civil unrest which led to civil war.

CHAPTER 2

CAPITAL PUNISHMENT

My mom no longer had a smile on her face or song on her lips. Her mouth twisted and deformed. When she spoke, it looked as though she talked out of the corner of her mouth.

Mom never hated anyone and trusted everyone. She was not a stupid woman, maybe, a little naïve. But there was something about my future bride, Delilah, that just made her uncomfortable. We had many conversations about her that always ended with mom telling me to pray about my relationship. There was nothing to pray about, she was pretty and rich. What more could I possibly want?

Mom passed away about six months before my wedding day. On her deathbed mom made a strange request to both dad and I. She made us promise never to receive a mark, on or under our skin, it would surely be the mark of Cain. It seemed silly, but, we both complied.

Mom left behind medical bills that were astronomical at best. Dad was in the process of losing the family home. I don't mean to sound vicious. Yes, I do. Where were all these church people and their promises of prosperity? Oh, a few came by with meals for dad and I. We could at least enjoy a hot meal, on a park bench, while our house got pulled out from under us.

Even the Pastor stopped by once. He rambled on about Mom being in a better place. I suppose if you consider a better place as being a graveyard with six feet of dirt stacked on top of a cold box, and not even a top of the line box, a better place. I guess he was right.

After mom's death dad started drinking a little more. Ahhh, that's bullshit, he became a flaming alcoholic. Not because he was losing the family home, he could care less. It was that mom was no longer there to enjoy it with him.

***

My bride, Delilah, came from a well to do family. In fact, her parents bought us a small two- bedroom ranch-style home in the burbs for a wedding present. It needed work but, I was pretty handy around the house.

Delilah's expensive taste was only exceeded by her vanity. Sure, she had faults but, who doesn't? Our wedding was nothing short of a Hollywood production. Her parents spared no expense. The reception, however, was a nightmare. Dad suffered a massive stroke. He recovered somewhat physically but, outside of a few obscure childhood memories, I could have been the paperboy, he wouldn't have known the difference.

I checked out a few nursing homes and they were so, so white. Oh, not the faculty, the walls, the ceilings, the floors all a blinding white. And the machines, pinging and ponging and looking like they came off a 1960's Sci-fi set. And the price, damn, I could put him up in a five-star hotel and gotten better service for the same cost.

Well everything comes down to the bottom line, and in this case, it was not money, it was my conscience. Here is a man who had taken care of me for over twenty years and I was ready to hide my shame in some home. No, no, no, that's not the way it's supposed to be. It was my turn to take care of him. We had a spare bedroom and, over Delilah's objection, Dad would move in.

It was hard but, we had to make it work. He had good days and he had bad days. It wasn't easy on him living with two strangers. Every once in a while, he would blurt out, "where's Becky?" That's about the only way I knew someone was at home between his ears. Dad mercifully passed away about a year after moving in.

My parents lived their lives as very frugal people. Actually, they did more existing than living. Dad's vacations were spent at home. I can count on one hand the number of times we went out to a restaurant. And pizza delivery was a treat. Yet, the financial world found its way into their lives and tried it's best to dis-hearten and destroy them. But their bond only got stronger. Then mom's God pulled the cruelest thing possible, he separated them. Well after dad passed away they had finally found a way to beat the system.

If I had learned anything from my parent's life, it was I was going to live not just exist. I probably maxed out more credit cards than the student body at the local college. And when it was my turn to die, I was going to die with a brand - new hummer in my driveway. As far as my body, they could roll me to the curb and I would be the street sweepers problem.

***

If there was a hell, that's the place my marriage was scripted. The only thing keeping me out of divorce court were the standards my parents had set. One of those standards was: when you make a choice, honor that choice. Believe me, I had made a lot of choices I latter regretted. My search for marital bliss was right at the top. To be fair, I can't put all the blame on Delilah's shoulders. We just lacked some sort of bonding agent and neither of us possessed the formula.

Over the years our life became a mundane and tragic relationship. I venture to say, it would rival an ancient Greek playwright's work. We were two individuals that happened to reside under one roof. I would plant myself in front of the TV or piddle with something around the house. Delilah would wrap herself in some book or workout with her headset tuned to classical music.

Conversation was not a form of communication. The only talking we did was to use phrases like "The dishwashers broken," or "Is dinner ready?"

Love making was an unsatisfactory experience. We engaged in sex three, maybe, four times a year, tops. And that was because she would tire of my constant badgering and sexual advances. If I led you to believe we made love, I must correct that assumption. Romance and I had gone our separate ways, long ago. It was more like, wham, bam, thank you mam. I would, rapidly, thrust my pelvis on her lifeless torso as she would file her fingernails or talk on the phone. When I finished my business, I would roll off of her totally disgusted with myself. I felt like some animal that had just conquered its basic primal carnal instinct. Damn, say that ten times real fast.

I do believe, I shall stop right there. I think, I said to much about my life of woes in the marriage of the damned.

Well it would be about eight years into my marriage when the World Health Care Reform Act went public and Lucas Cain's face was being plastered over various publications.

My wife was the trendy one. She would jump on any bandwagon that was popular at the time. And the Health Care act filled the bill. The Global Banking Network was the main sponsor of the program. The only identification the bank recognized was the "Goliath Chip." So, my wife received her ID implanted in her right thumb.

If it had been anyone but my Mother, I had made that vow to, years back, I would have searched, high and low, for some kind of loophole. But, because it was mom, a promise was a promise. As it was, I had an OK policy through the department, not great but, good.

For the next few years the world was business as usual. That is, if you consider war, famine, pestilence, hate, greed and terrorism the norm. Then yes, the world was running just fine.

***

Father David Gideon and Father Daniel Myles were best friends through college. Both educated by the Diocese and employed at the Vatican.

When Pope Hydarnes V came to power it became mandatory for all employees to be insured by the World Health Care Reform. Gideon and Myles fought the mandate claiming it was not of God to have anything inserted under their skin.

Everyone, they pleaded their case to, either slammed the door in their face or were told it would be looked into. Nothing ever came of their inquiries. Father Myles was far more vocal with his concerns. He threatened everything from boycotts to going public. We lived in a time when you did not piss off the hierarchy.

Early one morning Father David Gideon was aroused from sleep by the sound of sirens. As he opened his eyes the sight of red, blue and yellow lights danced on the walls making the room look more like a disco than a bed chamber. He donned his robe and slippers and went to investigate.

The door leading to Father Daniel Myles apartment was sealed off by the authorities and the large crowd that gathered outside made David's access to Daniel's apartment an impossibility. But, the word buzzing through the crowd was that Daniel had hung himself. That idea to David was ludicrous. It was here that David met Bishop Angelo de Leone. The Bishop requested David's presence in the garden, Angelo loved gardens.

Bishop de Leone sat amongst the beauty of the flowers waiting for David. To occupy his time he fed the pigeons, which had grown quite a sizable flock. Every once in a while, he would use his foot to move some of the more aggressive birds, allowing access to some of the timid birds.

David neared the bench where Angelo sat. Angelo never made eye contact and talked as though he were talking to himself or the pigeons. He, like David, did not believe Daniel's death a suicide. What did surprise David was that Angelo thought David would suffer the same fate. The Bishop did not Mince words and told David he needed to get out now! Angelo got up and slapped the bag of bird seed into David's chest and left.

The pigeons moved to David's feet waiting for some savory morsels, but David was too engrossed in thought to pay any heed. He knew nothing, why should anyone want him dead?

And then again why was Daniel dead? He got up and waded through the sea of birds, still oblivious to their presence, toward his residence.

He entered his abode and placed the bag of seed on his nightstand. He paced for a few minutes completely lost as what to do. He had one option, that was to consult the only one left he could trust. He knelt by his bed and asked guidance from God.

As he got up his foot kicked the nightstand and the bag of seed tumbled to the floor. It scattered everywhere. Among the pellets was a ticket to Israel, a note with a contact, named Deborah, and a wad of cash.

CHAPTER 3

THE WRITING IS ON THE WALL

I came out of the academy some fifteen years back shortly before my marriage. I was a brash young rookie with a big chip on my shoulder. I was going to clean up crime and corruption, in the Baltimore area, single handed. And if it meant taking down politicians or financial big wigs, all the better. Wyatt Earp step aside there's a new crime fighter in town.

It did not take long for the realities of the job to set in. It was nothing like TV. My days were filled with traffic stops or some childish misdemeanor. The paperwork involved with these petty busts, hardly made the infraction seem worth the trouble.

Once or twice a year I pulled traffic control for a parade, a bikeathon or some nonsense like that. The only thing these entities did was clog up traffic and frustrate motorists. It appeared to me like they broke the first rule of common sense, if you wish to endear someone to your cause, don't piss 'em off.

To make matters worse, nobody has respect for the badge or trust in the law. Everybody screaming police brutality. Its like we are interfering with their right to be molested or murdered.

A couple of years ago I was promoted to detective and things changed very little. My paycheck increased slightly and I didn't have to make sure I had a clean uniform. What thrilled me the most was I didn't have to deal with those damn parades.

I was partnered with a ten- year vet by the name of James "Red" McCleary. The man had a drinking problem. Of course, he called it social drinking while I had seen alcoholism before. Promptness was never one of his attributes which added credibility to my diagnosis. The only thing he lived for was clock-out time when he could make it to the local watering hole for happy hour. I could hardly put all the blame on him. He had about an eight- year head start on me to become disgruntled with the job.

On this particular day, my training and knowledge were finally being put to the test. It was a murder case but. The victim's name was Sarah Wright. Her body was discovered by her father, Chief Justice Randall Wright, at about 6 am when he came to pick her up for work.

Now, I had already been upstairs to view the body and now interviewing the Chief Justice. And true to form, my partner had not yet made his appearance.

It was obvious Randall Wright was in great distress and I did my best to decipher what he was telling me.

Sarah had been employed by BarTech industries. She lost her job a couple of years ago. What I found most intriguing was she was engaged to the lead scientist on the Goliath project in England. His name was Isaac Marzban. Anyway, Isaac was found dead in his home in much the same manner as Sarah. Isaacs death scared Sarah so much that she fled back to the States.

My main concern was the similarities in the MO. The person or persons that committed this heinous crime had to know both victims. And that brings family and friends into play. Possibly a disgruntled family member that took exception to Isaac being involved with a white woman. But, why cross international waters to kill her when she was no longer posed a threat. I was baffled.

All indications told me this case belonged in the hands of the FBI, CIA, Homeland security, Family Counseling, or anyone but a local detective. Well, my jurisdiction, my case, period.

"Red" finally showed up. My first instinct was to intercept him before he made it to the Chief Justice. That instinct proved correct as I smelled last night's festivities all over him as I got within three feet. I filled "Red" in on the case as I led him upstairs to view the body, not that he gave a rat's ass.

What we had in all likelihood was a crucifixion. Sarah was seated in a chair clad in bra and panties. The only thing holding her in the chair were two nails driven through her wrists that were attached to both sides of the door frame. Her right hand was missing its thumb. Her throat had been slit as evident by the dry blood that ran down her torso and pooled at her feet.

Written on the wall next to Sarah's body was some incoherent gibberish or symbols. I assumed it was scribbled with her blood. But, that couldn't be established for sure till the lab report came back.

The last thing I had to do was interview the neighbor next door. She was a lady who stood in her yard mumbling about the end of days as the officers went about their investigation. I did not think anything would come of my questioning. That is outside of calling for an ambulance to get her fitted for a strait jacket. But a good detective must go where any lead takes them, no matter how stupid it seems.

I did not need "Red" tagging along, making the situation worse by cracking wise at this woman's expense. I suggested "Red" get some coffee as I would handle the interview. What the hell, I had a 50/50 shot he would actually get coffee.

The crazy woman answered the door, Well, she resembled a woman. Her hair was stringy and matted. Black mascara running down her face. Her purple lipstick looked like it had been applied with a paint sprayer. Her eyes so blood-shot I could not tell their original color. Her raggedy house coat and slippers added to an unfavorable look that would have given "Red" more ammunition.

The room was smoke fill and it felt like I inhaled a pack of cigarettes before I made it to the sofa. An ash tray on the coffee table was overflowing and still smoldering. Next to the ash tray was half a bottle of scotch.

The lush still stuck to her, end of the world, story. But maybe, "Red" should have been here? Perhaps, he could interpret the language of slur better than I could?

As I was ready to leave, she grabbed me by the arm and started to lead me to the front window. I could not help but think, for an unkempt drunk, wearing a wardrobe straight off the rack of bag lady chic, she was kind of, sexy. I wondered what she would be like in the sack.

We reached the window and she released my arm to open the drapes. I snapped back to my senses. Ok Joel, get your mind out of the gutter and focus.

She pointed to a lamp post across the street. She claimed that at about 4AM she saw someone standing under it, having a cigarette. The person was dressed in black sweatpants and a black hooded sweatshirt. She believed they were on foot.

In my mind, anyone dressed like that in this heat was either on an extreme weight loss regiment or up to no good. I thanked her and left.

I crossed the street and surveyed the ground under the lamp post. There it was, a cigarette butt. I carefully picked it up and bagged it. I then assumed the person that was here was walking because, she saw no car. Now if the person was going south, he would not have bothered to cross the street. If he was going east, he would have chosen the lamp post on the other side of the house. So, this person's destination had to be within two blocks north northwest of the crime scene. At least, that's as far as I would walk, especially, as hot as it was.

CHAPTER 4

#MYBAD

had arrived at the station early the next morning and to my surprise "Red" was already there. He was at the dispatcher's counter flirting with Marge. Marge's body language dictated her definition of flirt and pester differed from "Red's."

I looked at my desk and it was cluttered with paperwork. Over the years I had honed my own filing system that I dubbed the SCAB system. It seemed to worked for me. The SC was the shit can file. This was the stack containing office memos or things like an invitation to some snot nosed kid's birthday. The A stood for attention. Anything pertaining to the job at hand. In this case Sarah Wright. The B was for bureaucratic. Any, time consuming nonsense, such as, parole violations or a court summons found their way here.

I start the sorting and ran across the autopsy report on Sarah. It told me nothing more than I had suspected. The crucifixion had taken place while she was alive. After the perp or perps had enough fun, her throat was slit and she bled out within minutes. It seemed whoever did this enjoyed their job way too much.

More sorting, "what's this?" An invitation to Sam and Jolene's first wedding anniversary, how sweet. I crumpled it up and file it. Send me another one in five years, that is if they're still together, and maybe I'll consider going, but, probably not.

More sorting, and I get a hit on the cigarette butt. The DNA on it belonged to a Carl Parkes. I pull him up on my data base. He lived in apartment 8C Of the Briar Ridge complex. That was a half a block north of the crime scene. He was a petty thief and drug addict. What caught my attention was, he was an FBI informant which probably kept him out of doing time. I hate fucken moles. They have no loyalties and would stab you in the back if the situation were to their advantage.

He did not fit the MO but, he was the only lead I had. I put in a call to Chief Justice Wrights office. If anyone could expedite a warrant, it was him.

I finished my sorting and went to get McCleary. I tore "Red" from his one - sided romance with Marge. She looked relieved as though I had just removed a boil from her ass.

Well anyway, Our, first stop was to the preacher. His expertise was in language translation and code breaking. He was not expecting us as he had already sent his report upstairs. I must have missed it or misfiled it. Hey, I didn't say my system was perfect.

"Since were here," I asked? "Can you give us the gist of the report?"

"It's an early form of Aramaic," said the preacher as he reached for his bible. Handing me the book he just said, "Mark 15 verse 34, last entry."

Well, after a few minutes of fumbling through the book, "Red," getting a little agitated, grabbed the bible from me. Within seconds he had his finger on the verse. Damn, McCleary knew his way around the bible better than me. It read, "My God, My God why have you forsaken me?" Great, I thought, a ritual slaying.

"Ok Joel, where to now," asked "Red?"

"Pick up a warrant," I replied.

"Wait a minute," said McCleary. "How did you get a warrant this quickly and by who's authorization?"

"Don't worry about it," I said.

"Damn it. Joel," he began, "you just don't jump over the chain of command without asking for trouble."

I was in agreement with him but, all we were going to do was look around and ask a few questions. If he had nothing to hide, well, no harm no foul.

"This one is on you, Joel," replied "Red." And that would be the last time he would address me by my given name.

We arrived about 11 AM and took the elevator to the eighth floor. We knocked on the door and announced who we were. There was no response. The door was open so we went in.

Parkes was on the phone and mumbled, "I can't go back to jail."

He darted towards the window and through the glass he went. I was almost certain he couldn't fly so, that left only one option. "Red" and I looked at each other for a moment, as if to say what the hell just happened. As soon as we got our focus back, we ran to the window.

Lying eight stories below in a pool of blood was Parkes. Arms and legs twisted, in a way, limbs were not intended to be twisted.

Down the stairs we went. McCleary checked the body for signs of life then called it in. meanwhile I scoured the area for Parke's phone. I found it, some of it in the grass, some of it under the dumpster and some of it on the cement.

McCleary told me we were ordered back to the station, now! But we had a dead body and I had not searched the apartment yet.

McCleary emphasized, "What part NOW does not compute?"

As we left, two black unmarked cars pulled near the body.

On the trip back to the station, I was being bombarded by words usually reserved for longshoremen or truck drivers.

The hustle and bustle became silence as we entered the squad room and all eyes fixated on us. That told me we were not in line for a pat on the back. I looked at Marge and she looked at the Captain's door. There he stood, much bigger than I remember.

I hardly got his door shut behind me when the verbal assault started again. The vocabulary didn't change, just the person spewing the words. The subject matter remained the same, Protocol, everything I had gotten an earful for the past hour. Sure, I messed up but, for crying out loud, I didn't push the son of a bitch out of the window.

When things simmered down, it came to light that we had just ruined months of an FBI investigation

When it came time for the blame game, I felt the noose tightening around my neck. Then "Red" pulled the lever that released the trap door.

McCleary got assigned to a desk job and I got suspended indefinitely. Suspended and indefinitely are two words you do not want to hear in the same sentence.

I got a double whammy that day. I not only lost my job, but I got to spend some quality time with Delilah, the queen of "not tonight I've got a headache."

CHAPTER 5

EENY – MEENY – MINY - MOE

The first week or so of suspension wasn't too bad, there was a lot of maintenance around the house to keep me occupied. But now, make work jobs were getting kind of scarce.

I resorted to watching a lot of TV. As I channel surfed, I passed up game shows that pitted contestants against each other for their knowledge of some off the wall trivia that has no value to anyone. I didn't need to know things like, why milk curdles as it sours? It just does. When common sense dictates don't drink or eat it, depending on what stage of the curdling process it is in, is all the answer required.

For lack of a better option, I stopped on a news special. It was a debate on the Carmichael Bill. It was a bill meant to bring sovereignty to America and freedom from the world's economic woes. It put exorbitant tariffs on imports and exports. This was to keep what's made in America, stays in America. The Federal Reserve was abolished to keep the economy from fluctuating.

On paper it was a noble gesture. In practical application, not so much. For starters, there were millions of people lobbying for a one world order. And since the heatwave and drought hit, many ranches and farms were going belly up and in need of Government assistance. But the money was not there. Major business was doing the opposite of what was expected. They were pulling up stakes and moving out. Unemployment was running rampant.

Peaceful protests and marches were turning into violent riots.

Oh well, not my problem, I had enough problems of my own.

***

After a while TV starts to lose its appeal for combating boredom. Perhaps, I'll paint the fence. It did not need it but, it was something to do. So, off I went to the hardware store for supplies.

On the way home, I stopped at Mickey's pub. I really didn't want to paint the fence. Three hours later, I made it home.

Delilah was at the table reading. She had on a t shirt and workout pants. She was still sexy. I had just enough beers in me to make my move on her. I started groping and fondling her as she fought back.

"Damn it, Joel, you smell like your dad," she yelled.

She sure knew how to kill a mood. A simple "get off of me" Would have had the same effect but, would have been less hurtful.

After I simmered down, she informed me someone had payed me a visit. His name was Bishop Angelo de Leone. He requested an audience with me at Our Lady of Sorrow. The information I needed was on the counter in the kitchen.

I really, really didn't want to paint the fence, and this, de Leone guy, peaked my interest. Besides I needed a little time away from the bitch. So, I grabbed the note and drove to Our Lady of Sorrow. I couldn't possibly understand what a high- ranking church official wanted with me. My questions would soon be answered as I pulled into the parking lot of the church.

Bishop de Leone met me there and insisted we go to the garden. The guy seemed fixated on gardens. It wasn't much of a garden, just a few blossoms.

"Are you a religious man, Joel," asked the Bishop?

After an uncomfortable silence the Bishop added, "I take it you are not."

Oh shit, I was trapped. It was like one of those uninvited, bible thumping, holy rollers had showed up at my door. At least with them you could pretend you are not at home or just slam the door in their face. But this was different, I was in his back yard with nowhere to run. I settled on looking at the ground and shaking my head no.

"It's probably to your advantage that you are not," the Bishop said. "What I have to tell you is something, I know, you will not want to hear, but, need to know."

Angelo de Leone took me back some 2000 years to the birth of Christianity and its charismatic leader. Back when it was a cult, if you will, an offshoot of Judaism. The Gentiles were sort of an outreach program.

Being basically a Jewish religion, the only laws they had were the Old Testament. Especially the Torah, or Book of Laws. The Gospels did not even start to be penned till some 50 years after the death of its founder.

The specific law the Bishop was referring to was found in the book of Leviticus Chapter 16, verses 8-10: Aaron casts lots for two goats, one for the Lord the other for the scapegoat. One was sacrificed for sin, the other released to Azazel in the wilderness.

"With the crucifixion of Christ," the Bishop started. "For the law to be fulfilled, the scapegoat had to be released. Pilate fulfilled that obligation by setting free the prisoner Barabbas, the adversary or better known as the Anti - Christ."

"Wait a minute, what the hell is an Anti – Christ and what has he to do with me," I inquired?

"He is the mirror image of Christ, the complete opposite and your adversary," said the Bishop.

"Let's see if I have this straight," I said. "Your telling me that some 2ooo year old man, I don't even know, is out gunning for me."

"The age of the man is not relevant, but yes you have the gist of it," said Angelo.

I considered Bishop Angelo de Leone an honorable man maybe, a little over zealous in his beliefs. But I was a cop and could not go on here say. I needed reliable proof.

The Bishop told me another story. About five years ago he had been on a tour of France and wished to meet, this miracle worker, Cardinal Lucas Cain. The Bishop was greeted by Father Alexander Gray. The Bishop knew Gray from the past, when Gray's faith was wavering and solitude was his desire. But now Gray was outgoing and personable. A complete, turn around.

Cain and Angelo talked for a while. The Bishop could not help but notice the birthmark on the back of Cardinal Cain's right hand. It looked like one of those spinning lawn ornaments from a distance. When they shook hands to say goodbye, the Bishop noticed the birthmark was a cluster of three sixes. From that day forward the Bishop has followed the actions of both, Cain and Gray.

"Still not enough, sir, I need more," I said.

With a straight face, Angelo said, "God has chosen you."

I let out a belly laugh. "I'm sorry, Padre, I'm not laughing at you, I'm laughing at the idea. Why would this God of yours choose a man like me?"

"I don't know," he replied. "Why would he choose Noah, a drunk? Why would he choose Moses, a murderer and man with low self-esteem? Why would he choose King David, an adulterer? Perhaps someday you can ask him yourself."

"Let's go under the assumption that you are right," I began. "Just for shits and giggles, excuse the language, after the devastation your God had brought upon my family, why would I consider doing anything he requests of me."

"Because God does not ask," he said as he got up and started to walk away. "It's been a pleasure meeting you, Joel."

I sat there for a moment trying to dismiss the insanity, I had just heard, and organize the days events. This has, definitely, not been one of my better days.

CHAPTER 6

TO SERVE THE MASTER

Today was the day I fulfill my obligation to myself and paint the fence. It will be tough because of the extreme heat. And I can't remember the last time we had precipitation of any kind. Since the heatwave hit the daily, worldwide, death toll was on the rise. The recipients were mainly the poor, the elderly and the weak. By weak, I mean people of faith. Those depending on this imaginary God to get them through the crisis. Even if this Higher Power existed, it was pretty apparent this entity cared nothing about the human condition.

It was spring yet, the scene looked like the middle of winter. The trees barren of foliage and the grass a brownish beige. There were a couple spots of greenery fighting a losing battle for life.

Between hydration breaks and rest from the heat, it was dark by the time I finished. I was tired and hungry. I laid everything on the porch. I'll clean it up tomorrow.

The first thing I saw entering the house was my wife Delilah sitting on the sofa. She was clad in a white teddy. Her breasts pushing against the shear material, leaving very little to the imagination.

She was sitting with her legs tucked up underneath her and a glass of wine in her hand. She looked terrific for a broad in her upper thirties. Behind her, the lights were dimmed and the table lit by a center piece of candles.

I went over to give her a hug and a kiss.

"Shower first, Joel" she said.

I was naked before I reached the bathroom. I didn't want to give her time to sober up or come to her senses.

In the bathroom there was no towels so I went out to the closet to get one. She was talking to someone. I thought, please no visitors tonight and peeked around the corner. Delilah was on the phone. I let out a sigh of relief.

I finished my shower, quickly, anticipating a little dinner and an evening of passion. This time with a twist, it would be consensual on both sides. That should have sent up a red flag but, I was thinking somewhere below my belt. Because of the heat, I slipped into a pair of silk boxer shorts and nothing else. I reasoned it was ok because Delilah was half naked herself.

When I came out of the bathroom, I was surprised to see two, filled, wine glasses. One by my spot at the head of the table. At least, I'll call it the head in theory. And the other glass on her side. And that did send up a red flag.

To comprehend, you must understand my wife. At dinner time she was very prim and proper. A ritual I blame on her parents. It took her a long time to break me of my, plop my ass in front of the TV and eat with my fingers, habit.

Well anyway, the first course was either soup or salad. I always hoped for soup. If it was salad, I had the dilemma of two forks. I had to hope I selected the right one or risk a scolding from Delilah.

The entrée came out next. I always loved it when the rolls were by her. She would bring the whole basket to me, just, so I could pick one. It would have been, so much, easier to grab one and send it to me air mail. The butter would have been a different story. I'm getting off track, here, but getting a chuckle out of good memories.

Desert was next on the menu. And then, we would retire to the living room for wine, a cordial or coffee.

Now, the one thing you never did, I mean never ever did, was come to the table in your underwear. When I unintentionally, sat down in my boxers and did not get read the riot act, oh yes, something was way out of whack.

"Can you get some cheese, sweetheart?" I can't remember the last time I used that term of endearment.

"Yes; cheese," she replied. She slowly and robotically turned and went to the kitchen.

I couldn't take it, what the hell was wrong with her? While she was gone, I switched our wine glasses. I don't know why? I just did. Perhaps it was just an uncomfortable feeling I had. Nothing was as it should be.

Delilah returned and we sat there sipping our wine. She just stared at me with this vacant emotionless look. In all the years we had been together, I had never seen her that hammered.

Suddenly, she began to swooned and her eyes rolled up into her head. I jumped up and caught her before she passed out on the floor. I carried her to the sofa and laid her down. The sheer material of her skimpy Teddy allowed all of her private parts to stare me in the face. Alas, there would be no sex tonight. UNLESS! Ohh, don't even think about you pig.

Decency won out and I headed to the bedroom to get dressed. As I headed to the bedroom, Delilah's phone rang.

"WHAT!" There was only silence on the other end. "Who is this," I asked? Still silence. I looked and it was an unknown number. Questions kept rising as I threw her phone. What was going on tonight, was there some kind of full moon out. I would probably get no answers from Delilah, she was so shit faced, she wouldn't remember anything, anyway.

I got dressed hoping that would give her time to come around. When I returned to the couch, Delilah's face was pale, her lips were a bluish purple and froth was bubbling out of the side of her mouth, down her cheek. I checked her pulse and breath, there was no sign of life. I performed CPR, but it was no use she was gone.

As I searched for my phone, I heard a car pull into my driveway. I looked through the blinds and saw it was a squad car. The passenger got out slowly. He was dressed to the nines. He placed a hat on his head, stretched and surveyed the neighborhood.

The driver, however, jumped from the car, pistol drawn and racing towards my front door. I recognized him as "Red." I didn't know what to expect, but it didn't appear he was here to exchange pleasantries, So I made a dash for the back door.

I heard my front door get kicked in as I entered the garage. I started my car and threw it in reverse, never bothering to open the garage door. I rammed the car in my driveway. My tires smoking and screeching as I shoved the vehicle into the street.

As I shifted into drive, I glanced at the man standing on my lawn. If death had a face, he was wearing it. And he had the most, evil smile I had ever seen.

I was too tired and hungry to think. I found a flea bag of a motel off the beaten track and pulled into the back of the parking lot, out of the sight of the road.

I pulled my drop gun from the glove box. My drop gun was a sort of insurance policy. If I happened to killed an unarmed criminal in the performance of a, criminal act, I would simply put the gun in his hand. It would save a lot of embarrassing questions at an inquest. Don't get all righteous on me, I never used it thus the reason I still have it. I went in to register.

There was a diner next door to the motel, I got a burger and fries. I was very careful to pay everything in cash till I can get a handle on the situation.

CHAPTER 7

BE CARFULL WHAT YOU WISH FOR

looked at the clock and it was 4:30 AM. I did not get much sleep but I felt alright. I would start by paying a visit to Bishop Angelo de Leone at Our Lady of Sorrow.

I couldn't take my car so I looked for one I could hotwire. I wasn't going to steal it, just borrow it.

I arrived at Our Lady of sorrow. There was one other vehicle in the parking lot. I pulled in next to it and went to the front door of the church and as luck would have it, it was open.

The sanctuary was rather large. "Hello," I said in a voice a little louder than normal conversation. "Is anyone here?"

A tap on my shoulder startled me and I turned Quickly almost drawing my weapon. An elderly priest stood behind me.

I requested to see Bishop de Leone. Well the only de Leone he had heard of died a few months back in Rome. He asked if there was, anyway, he could help.

I was a little depressed and shook my head, no.

I slumped into a pew to rethink another strategy. Where to go from here? I could start with Sarah Wright's neighbor. Damn, I felt her so unreliable, I never got her name. I knew where she lived but getting there was going to be a challenge. My cash was running low and using my card was not an option, without putting my location at risk.

Moments later the man emerged from the other room dressed in civilian clothes. "Leave your car here, we'll take my van," he had said as he rushed past me. "I'm Father Thomas Riley."

"Joel Braxton," I replied following him out the door.

We headed north up 95. "Where are we going," I asked?

"Delaware," he replied. "We need to get you somewhere safe till we get this sorted out."

"Do you mind using the cash only lanes," I asked?

"What kind of trouble are you in son," Riley inquired?

"It's complicated."

"Try me," he replied. "Let's start with this person claiming to be Bishop Angelo de Leone."

I explained my conversation with this, so called de Leone guy.

"Do you have any enemies," Riley asked?

"I'm a cop, I have many enemies," I began. "But, outside of my wife, none that had made an attempt on my life."

"Oh, your wife. Are you up to going there?"

It was personal and hard. I tried to relate the events leading to the death of my wife, Delilah.

"Was your wife a member of the World Health Care Reform," Father Riley asked?

I nodded in the affirmative.

Well, it appeared, that in a survey of members of Health Care act most were in favor of a One World Order. It was like a compulsion. He likened it to a smoker trying to quit. Without a strong will and inner strength, chances of success were minimal. Then he added that a device that strong could conceivably be capable of harboring a post hypnotic suggestion. Most likely triggered by an outside source, such as a voice on her phone.

All Father Riley told me was logical, yet, it did not answer the questions of who would put a contract on my head and why?

The trip took about an hour and half. We pulled into a small parking lot of a church in Dover.

In the basement of the church there were all sorts of radios, TV monitors, computers and a world map on the wall with all sorts of colored stick pins covering it. I had never seen a war room, but, if I were to imagine one, this would be it. I see nothing that eases my fear that I may be in the midst of terrorists. I'm in enough trouble as it was, I did not need that scenario tacked on.

Father Riley excused himself and left the room. The only other person in the room was a man on a computer. He looked busy and I did not want to disturb him so, I would entertain myself. I focused on the map with all the stick pins. I knew not what I was looking at. I was just killing time.

A tap on my shoulder startled me and I turned abruptly. As soon as my heart settled down, I noticed, it was the man who was at the computer. His name was Yechezk'el, with a last name I can pronounce, but there are so many consonants in it, it would be hard to verbalize in print. So, I'll just call him, Ezekiel or Zeke.

Zeke was a Professor of History at DU, specializing in Ancient Linguistics. He had shoulder length dark hair, wire rimmed glasses, jeans with holes all over and sandals on his feet. He looked more like, what my grandparents would call, a hippie than a dignified Professor.

"I noticed your interest in our map," said Zeke.

"Just curious about all these colored stick pins." I answered.

"Allow me to ease your mind," Zeke started. "The white pins indicate the movements of the Anti – Christ."

"Please, can we talk about unicorns, I asked sarcastically? "I just, can't buy into this Anti – Christ bullshit."

"What's so hard to believe," he asked? "You've, probably, been dancing with his boss your whole life."

"Point taken, I'll shut up and listen," I replied.

Zeke pointed to the board. "All these red pins are worldwide war zones. These black ones are pestilence and famine. And the beige pins are death. All together they are, better known as, the four horsemen of the apocalypse."

I was true to my word and kept silent. But I could not help but think, had this guy been on an extended vacation from planet earth?

Everything he told me has been going on since mankind came into the picture. Well, who am I to burst his bubble?

"The blue ones are disasters," said Zeke.

"Why are there so many in California," I inquired?

It seems last night, while I was busy saving my sorry ass, a massive earthquake shook the whole State causing major destruction and death. The ramifications split the State, almost, to the Oregon border.

Suddenly a door opened and Father Riley came back in accompanied by a young woman. She was the most infatuating creature I had ever laid eyes on. If there was such a thing as the perfect woman, she was the model.

"It's nice to see you again, Joel," said the woman.

I did not hear a word she said.

"My eyes are up here, Joel," she said with a smile. "You don't remember me, do you?" "Lily Faraday?" "Come on Joel, Sarah Wright's, next door neighbor?"

Oh, the lush, I thought, I reached out to shake her hand. Suddenly I had this vision of the two of us, our naked bodies, entwined in uninhibited taboo fornication, under the stars.

"Can I have my hand back," she asked?

I released her hand, almost, apologetically and embarrassed as if she knew what I was thinking. My wife's body isn't even cold yet and here I am wanting to bed down someone else.

She had to leave but, her advice to me was to listen to what Zeke had to tell me. So, I returned to the map with all the pretty colored stick pins.

"I know she's a looker," said Zeke. "But, please focus on what I am Saying and it does concern you."

"Satan has a lease on Planet Earth and that lease is expiring," Zeke began. "The document is bound by seven seals. The first four seals have been broken, thus, the pins on the map."

"Just for the sake of argument," I said. "I don't see what that has to do with me. Isn't that dispute between your God and Satan?"

"I see you're a hard sell," said Zeke. "Ok; humanity, and that includes you, are also tenants and subject to the same terms of the lease. Follow? What is going on around you is the Landlord rectifying the damage his tenants have done. Like it or not, Joel, you are part of the process."

All this was too much to wrap my head around. I was in trouble and there was nothing, I could see, that was supernatural about it. I needed to be alone to sort through all the nonsense and gather the pertinent information.

Zeke pointed to the other room. "Take all the time you need," he said.

It seems, to me, I have a few alternatives. One is: these people have taken symbolic biblical references and materialized them. But nothing going on indicates anything of a supernatural nature. The extreme heat is simply the Earth's orbit had shifted a little closer to the sun. The drought was because; because. Well, I'm no scientist, but there must be a logical explanation. The earthquake that shook

California. Let's just say, they lived on a fault line, what the hell did they think was going to happen? As far as the Devil is concerned, I'll suffice to say, the only devils I knew were locked away, in padded rooms, in some asylum, somewhere.

Another alternative was: these people were out of their frigging minds. I suppose, though, anyone that didn't think as I thought or believed as I believed had to be nuts, anyhow.

The last, remote, alternative was that I was the butt end of some elaborate practical joke. That seemed, to me, a lot of wasted time and energy, on a prank, just to jump out and say, "GOTCHA."

"Hmm GOTCHA, is that even a word? Solomon has everything in this briefcase except a dictionary. Well I hold the pen, so I say it's a word."

It's obvious that I am getting nowhere, fast.

All I have to go on are the facts. Fact 1: My wife is dead. Fact 2: I was involved in a hit and run, with a squad car no less. Fact 3: I borrowed a car without permission. Fact 4: There are, most likely, warrants out on me, on all counts. Which leads to fact 5: It would not have been the Devil signing those warrants.

It's decision time? I could walk out of this looney bin and wander the streets, aimlessly, not knowing what I am looking for. That's kind of a bad idea. I would probably be picked up in a couple days, I'm not that clever. When I got picked up, they could add another charge: carrying an unregistered weapon. But, until I get some satisfactory answers, this gun stays with me till death we do part.

The only option I had left was less appealing. I would remain and try to sort this puzzle out. This was the hardest case I've ever had. The difference being, I am now the fugitive.

CHAPTER 8

TO SPEAK WITH FORKED TONGUE

The first thing that needed to be done was to get my identity changed. All my documents were changed to my mother's maiden name, Pethuel.

I still had to work. These cells had a vast network of family, friends and business partners that would employ on a cash only basis. They did not pay much but, at least, it would give you a sense of self - worth and some integrity. A character builder, if you will. Who the hell am I kidding? I would have had to claw my way back up, to reach the bottom of the food chain.

Over the next few months, civil war had broken out in America. Unlike the war of the 1860's, this time outside influences had taken advantage of America's weakened condition and the invasion had begun.

This should be no surprise. If history had taught us anything, it's the life expectancy of a Super Power is only a few hundred years. You would have thought, after all the centuries, someone would have figured out what went wrong and rectified the situation. But, I suppose, as long as there is squabbling in the ranks and discontent among the masses, well, you do the math.

During this time Zeke had taken me under his wing as my mentor in the daily operations and chain of command.

The Governing bodies of these cells were basic and efficient. The many cells, worldwide, were broken into seven chapters. Each chapter was headed by a flagship, or candlestick as it was called. The candlestick kept each member in its chapter informed of current events. It was also the strategic command center.

All of the candlesticks were under the jurisdiction of a central hub, known as the chandelier. But everyone knew this hub as "Doomsday John."

Well anyway, more importantly than being my instructor, Zeke had become my friend. And friendships for a man like me was a rare commodity. It requires a certain amount of trust. A trait I had lost, forgotten and no longer in my vocabulary.

I think what drew me to Zeke was his demeaner. I had always envisioned professors as stuffy old farts that stunk of education. He was nothing like that, He had a great sense of humor. He understood, shit happens and sometimes it can't be controlled. Sometimes you just have to smile and roll with the punches. We both spoke the same language but, Zeke showed more restraint expressing it. All in all, I believed we were on the same page.

"Excuse me for a moment, I think I got Writer's cramp in my fingers."

***

"Ok that's better, I'm back".

One afternoon, Lily came bearing bad news. It seems many cells in the Eastern Hemisphere were being sought out and eliminated. With the war now on American shores, she thought our little safe house would, also, be compromised.

Therefor we began bug out procedures. That's where you move to a new location and anything you can't take, with you, must be destroyed.

The procedure is not as easy as it sounds. Most of the people had outside jobs and families, they could not, just, uproot. They could remain at the original cell. But, when danger was imminent, they had a flight and destruction protocol.

Then, there were the few known as the live-ins. We were the ones that sought sanctuary from the outside world. Zeke had no family and could easily commute to work, so he chose to be a live-in. Bug out for live-ins was no big deal.

Our new Headquarters was a Cathedral in Philadelphia. Well, not exactly the building. There was a mausoleum in the grave yard behind the structure. It came with a trap door that led underground.

I could not believe what I was looking at. These caverns were gigantic. And they came with all the comforts of home. It seems, this place must have been under construction for years preparing for this moment in time.

Day by day our once spacious domain was getting smaller and smaller. Many cells along the eastern seaboard were fearing for their safety and seeking sanctuary. Philadelphia was the recipient of this movement.

***

It was early November and all of our monitors and radios were tuned to the Vatican Network. The Pope was going to give an address to the state of the world. Well, it was more of a bash on Christianity. I don't remember the speech word for word, so I'll jot down the gist of what I recollect.

He started by putting a doubt on the very existence of this Christ person. The Pope claimed, that Christ was a figment of an over-zealous imagination. Created by a people in desperate need of a Savior.

He justified that statement with logic and common sense. His oratory went on, that a man, who people, said performed so many miracles, including raising the dead and raising himself from the dead, well, he would be the most popular man on earth. Yet, Ancient records make no mention of this miracle worker.

The only place this man was given credibility was the Bible. Therefore, if this man did not exist then the Bible was a book of blasphemy and lies.

It was mandated, that anyone reading or in possession of this book would be charged with heresy. The penalty for such a crime would be public impalement. And the body would remain on display as a deterrent for such blasphemy.

I could not help but wonder, has the world gone back a few hundred years to a time when witch hunts were a popular form of entertainment. But wait, it does not get any better.

Anyway, since this Christ person never existed, all who were born again in his name were not saved and damned to eternity in the inferno. To rectify the situation, animal sacrifices were re-instated. In lieu of an animal, money could be sent to the Vatican for eradication of sin on a monthly basis. The money part made it seem a little less barbaric. Now, turning in a heretic would be enough of a sacrifice to forgive your sins for life.

That speech taught me a couple of things about the man. He mixed truth with lies. The man was a con artist, a very good one but a BS artist, none the less. Secondly by attacking anything, that makes you fear that object. And fear makes you vulnerable.

CHAPTER 9

GOD'S PET

There was an elite Army known as the Military Armed Ground Offensive Galaxies on the pay role of the GBN. There were thirteen of these Galaxies, each ten thousand troops strong. The strategic commander of all the Galaxies was General Ogden Gehrhardt.

The main purpose of these Galaxies was to move into war torn countries, establish marshal law and set up the new regime.

Intel had it that, at least, one of these Galaxies was planning on invading Israel with Gehrhardt, himself, at point. That poses as a major problem. A woman by the name of Esther St. Croix had sanctuary status at the cell in Israel. But sanctuary means nothing to a people that are out for her blood. The only option was someone had to retrieve Esther and bring her back to America.

"It is dangerous, Joel but, with your background in law enforcement, I would like you to go get Esther and bring her back," asked Lily?

To me it was a no brainer. I had been cooped up for such a long time, that danger or not, I needed to get out.

This would be the last time Lily and I laid eyes on each other.

***

We had chosen Thanksgiving Eve as my departure day. I would be able to blend in with the rest of the Holiday travelers. Besides, with the war going on, the Government had more important things to worry about than the likes of me.

The original plan was to land at El Prat airport in Barcelona. From there I needed to board a single prop or small twin-engine aircraft. The small make shift runway, tucked in the hills, could not handle anything larger than these small puddle jumpers. But, like all plans, there was a glitch.

The civil war in Spain was getting messy and a safe landing could not be guaranteed. The flight was redirected to Egypt. From there the plan would be back on track.

The landing in Israel was an adventure in itself. We bounced over the ruts and rocks of the landing strip. It was both terrifying and had the feel of an amusement park ride. Hell, when we came to a stop, I was not sure if we were still on the runway.

I was met at the door by young woman. "Joel, I presume," she asked? "Please come in, someone will be with you shortly."

The first thing I noticed upon entering was a stench in the air. I looked along the baseboards and in the corners for some kind of dead animal. When I discovered none, all I could think was these people needed to find the soap and water a little more often. Especially in these close quarters.

I saw a woman sitting by the coffee machine. She seemed uninterested in all the activity going on around her.

I poured a cup of coffee and asked her if she would like one?

"No thank you, monsieur," she said as her gaze trailed off to the floor.

In order to hear her soft- spoken babble, I had to bend over and get as close to her mouth as I could.

It was at that point, I felt a tap on my shoulder, and turned with a start. Damnit, I wished people would stop doing that!

They were Mr. and Mrs. Graham from England. They had been on Holiday, as they called it. And soon found out Jerusalem was not the vacation mecca its brochures claimed. For that day they acted as my interpreters. But, I swear, with their strong accent and pronunciation of the Queens English, sometimes I felt I needed an interpreter to interpret them.

It seemed that the young wallflower by the coffee machine was, indeed, Esther St. Croix. The one I was to escort back to the States.

The Grahams gave me a background on her. A few years back, she was a nun. In a moment of indiscretion, she had been impregnated by a young priest. Esther never divulged the fathers name. She chose not to ruin two lives. During her pregnancy, she had been counselled by Father Alexander Gray. When it came time for delivery, instead of a hospital, Father Gray took her to a warehouse. Bishop de Leone had been suspicious of both Gray and Cain. He followed Gray to the warehouse. When he saw that the baby was to be sacrificed, he panicked. But the baby was a stillborn, God had beaten them to the punch. Still needing a sacrifice, attention was shifted to Esther. If the authorities even believe the Bishop, it would take too much time to get there. So, he did the only thing he could think of, he pulled the fire alarm. In the chaos that ensued, the Bishop got Esther out and shipped her here, where she has been since.

As far as I could see, the only sin Esther is guilty of is getting knocked up. And that sure wasn't grounds to warrant a lynch mob.

Iyov Melchizedek was the newly appointed leader of the cell. He replaced Deborah when she and one of her companions defied the Pope's bible ban and passed out bibles on the streets of Jerusalem. As far as I knew, their bodies were still on display in the town square.

Iyov was an old school Jew and spoke no English. He was picked because the others felt Iyov had the favor of God. At one time he had a large ranch. In the village where he lived, he was an Elder and community leader. His advice was sought after and treasured.

The enemy, my new companions called evil forces, saw the value in such an influential man. They did all they could to win Iyov's allegiance but, to no avail. When bargaining proved futile, they resorted to intimidation. First the enemy seized his land and animals. Iyov stuck to his guns. His sons and daughter were murdered. Still Iyov held fast to his convictions.

If this man had the favor of God, something was wrong? All I know is if this God of Iyov wanted to favor me... I wished he would not. I had enough on my plate without this entity giving me another helping.

Anyway, with Iyov was his loyal wife, Salome. She only addressed her husband. She struck me as a woman who would walk three or four paces behind her man.

Also, among this abode's dwellers was Jael, the woman that allowed me entry. She was the granddaughter of Iyov and Salome. She seemed highly educated and well versed in the English language. Fact is, she put my butchery of the language to shame.

The thing about Jael was she was nothing like her grandparents. She was rebellious and outspoken. She fit the mentality of the women's lib movement. I saw her as being one of the first in line to throw her bra on the pyre.

The war was raging on in Spain but, that was not these peoples concern at this time. What did concern them was that a group of terrorists had seize the opportunity to attack the Embassy and take the Ambassadors hostage. Among them being held was Jael's husband, Solomon Heber.

Father David Gideon, remember him. Well, he had been working on a rescue mission with the Spanish Government. It was a time consuming, effort just to find the right soldiers for the job. To qualify, you could not have an identification chip in your thumb. Next your loyalties had to be with in-term Government. And finally, you had to be an expert marksman.

In the end they found 300 soldiers that fit the bill. The plan was now ready to be put into action.

CHAPTER 10

TO SERVE THE MASTER (PART 2)

The leader of the terrorist organization was Major Carlos Sisera, a power hungry, cold-blooded tyrant with no values put on human life. He ruled by fear, which he mistook for respect. If he had one weakness, it was beautiful women and Jael fit that profile.

She gained entrance to the mansion under the guise of a gift to Sisera for all of his success procuring the Embassy. Her low-cut, thigh high red dress molded to every curve of her voluptuous body. Her long dark hair cascaded over her shoulders. And the three- inch stiletto heels enhanced her shapely legs. Her disguise did exactly what it was intended to do. Get Sisera thinking with his penis.

One of the guards got a bottle of wine and two glasses while the other inspected Jael's bag. The guard put a smile on his face. She had enough sex toys to supply a small orgy.

Sisera would handle the body inspection upstairs. After all, there was no where to conceal a weapon with what she was wearing.

Sisera grasped the neck of the bottle and held the stems of the glasses between his fingers, in one hand. With the other hand he guided Jael up the stairs using her ass as the steering wheel. While going up she wiggled and quick stepped trying to avoid the touch of the slime ball. He was so arrogant, he believed Jael actually enjoyed his company.

In the room he set the wine and glasses on the dresser. Then he returned to his assault on Jael.

"Hold on Senor, let me get ready," she said.

She squirmed to get herself in position. She gently walked him back to the bed and gave him a playful nudge. He plopped down sitting on the edge of the bed. She returned to the dresser, opened the wine and poured two glasses.

With her back to him, she unlatched her ring and dumped a powdery substance in one of the drinks. She turned and brought that one to Sisera. She blew him a kiss and went to the bathroom.

Sisera sat there drinking his wine. When he had finished, he stood up to get another glass. He got dizzy and sat back down. The room was blurry and spinning. He made another attempt to stand but, this time he dropped the glass to the floor and fell back onto the bed in a prone position.

Jael emerged from the Bathroom The only thing she wore was a smile. She slid her arm up the doorframe and struck a seductive pose.

"Are you ready," She asked? She got no reply.

She dropped her arm and headed towards the bed. Her hair, breasts and muscles dancing to the rhythm of her stride. The low light from the nightstand lamp made her bronze body glisten as though it were freshly oiled.

She reached her destination and with a little force spun his legs onto the bed. She went to the dresser and pulled all the toys out of her bag and opened a false bottom. She took out a mallet and a railroad spike.

Returning to Sisera she placed the sharp end of the spike to his temple and with a mighty swing of the mallet drove the spike through his temple. The blood splattered on the bed, the walls and of course Jael.

She wiped the blood from the mallet on the sheets. She put it back on the dresser and went back to the bathroom. She climbed into the shower. The blood washed away easily and swirled down the drain. The shame, not so much.

She dried herself and got dressed. She combed her hair and applied her makeup. She stepped back from the mirror to make sure she was presentable. She gave her dress a tug at the hips along with a little wiggle. It would have to do.

Now she had to get out, she packed her bag. She tried to maintain a calmness as she moved down the staircase to the front door. Just as she reached for the knob.

"Un Momento," said the guard who had inspected her bag when she entered. He then walked towards her, while the other guard pumped his arms and gyrated his hips in some sort of stupid looking mating ritual.

The guard, walked up to her, bent over and whispered in her ear. "The sonny beech, how you say... he ease dead...Si?"

Jael nodded in the affirmative.

As he closed the door behind her, an explosion at the embassy rocked the mansion. The concussion shook the pictures on the wall, rattled the windows and started a chorus of clinking from the crystal and bottles on the shelves.

Ok, ok, you caught me. How could I know all the details, I wasn't there? All I had to go on was the outline Jael cared to share with me. I just filled in the blanks as I saw her evening going down. I guess, that makes me a gossip? Go ahead and add me to the list, I don't care.

CHAPTER 11

TIME TO GO HOME

I was sore and every joint in my body ached. The cots in this cell were not meant for a 6' 2" 210 + pound body frame. I could not worry about my pain, for today Esther and I would return to my stomping grounds in the U S of A. I continued packing but, something was missing and I couldn't put my finger on it.

David Gideon and Iyov had been occupied in conversation most of the morning. Iyov then entered his prayer room and was in there a long time.

I finished my packing and started helping Esther to expedite her slow movement. There was no telling how long our window of opportunity would remain open.

That's it!! Where are the Grahams? That was the uneasy feeling I had.

I made the mistake of inquiring about the Graham's where abouts from David Gideon. Now, David's English was terrible, at best. And he felt it necessary to use hand gestures, as though it made him understandable. I sympathized with his efforts but, on the other hand, he was kind of fun to watch. Well anyway, since I didn't have time for a game of charades, I picked out a couple of words I recognized. The words were, called and home. I assumed that meant the British Embassy had got them back to England.

Iyov finally emerged from his prayer room.

"You; Esther; Go. Jael; Solomon; Barcelona, understand?" David said struggling with his English.

"We; all; Go," I said. Shit, now I'm talking like David, hand signals and all.

David is now getting a little frustrated with his communication skills. "We," he said gesturing to Iyov and Salome. "Me," he said pounding his chest. "Stay," he said pointing at the floor. "I loose fate, understand?" He said. "Iyov Rabbi, understand?"

As near as I could decipher, he had lost faith and Iyov would be his teacher in regaining it.

"Iyov; teach you; America," I said.

David is now, obviously, perturbed. He turns to Iyov and begins speaking Hebrew.

Iyov unbuttons his shirt and throws it open. There was that stench I had smelled upon my entrance to the cell. Only this time more pungent. I reached into my pocket and pulled out my handkerchief. I stepped back about three feet and covered my nose and mouth. It was not very polite but, vomiting all over his shoes was the only other alternative.

Iyov's torso was wrapped in bandages. The bandages were covered red, yellow and green pus, some dry and some still oozing.

I could not imagine what purulent sores lie beneath and truly, didn't want to.

"You; Esther; Go," said David.

***

The airport in Barcelona was sparsely populated. There was a noticeable presence of many armed soldiers walking the perimeter and terminals. Esther and I were shuttled through baggage claim, around security and outside to our waiting air transport.

Jael and her husband Solomon were standing outside of the airplane. Apparently, there was a change in plans. It looked as though we would have two more passengers. Jael saw that her grandparents were not with us and rushed toward us. She inquired as to where they were.

"Not coming," I said.

"I will not go without them," she replied.

"I have a job to do," I replied. "What you do is your affair."

Solomon took Jael aside and talked to her. Moments later they linked arms and Solomon said, "Shall we go." Arm in arm, they climbed the stairway to the aircraft.

Outside of our small group, there were about thirteen other passengers. So, we could just pick our spot. I chose a seat at the back of the cabin in the middle of the center section. There I had a view of the whole cabin.

Jael and Solomon were a few rows up. They embraced and snuggled like a pair of starstruck teenagers in a disgusting display of affection. Or maybe, I was just a little jealous of their fairy tale relationship.

The cabin had a few passengers and many empty seats. So, choosing one was not a problem.

Esther had a back seat across the aisle from me. She just stared out of the window. I could not imagine what was going on in her head and really didn't want to.

Jael got up and came to the back. She sat down next to me and wanted to explain her actions at Sisera's mansion. I don't know if she was trying justify herself or just trying to relieve her conscience. Either way, I was tired and not interested. I just smiled and nodded a lot.

Jael got up and started back to her seat. My head moved to the sway of her gorgeous ass. Come on, she was hot and I wasn't dead.

Suddenly, the gentle hum of the aircraft's engines, were drowned out by the sound of thunder, lightning and torrential rain that pummeled the airplane.

We hit a turbulent pocket and the plane shimmied. I fastened my seat belt. Another turbulent pocket, another shimmy. With each shimmy, the aircraft gave the impression of splitting at the seams. With the situation out of my control, I settle for white Knuckling the arm rests.

Apparently, I wasn't the only one ready to shit their pants. At the front of the cabin, three men were huddled in, what looked like a prayer session. When they turned towards the back of the plane, the whole scenario changed. In place of faces, each man had a ram's head. The one in front, carried an engraved knife, which looked like a sacrificial dagger. They came towards me.

Instinctively, I reached for my weapon. I realized that I could not fly with it. I then tore at the buckle of my seat belt, as the men got closer. Damn multi-million-dollar aircraft and the seat belts are broke.

They reached the back. The men turned their attention to Esther and surrounded her. I stretched for them but, they were out of my reach. I saw the dagger raise in the air and then plunge down again and again. Each stroke spattered blood everywhere. I'm clawing at air.

"NOOOOOOOOO!!"

"This is your Captain…"

Damn, I must have dozed off. I quickly glance over to Esther. She gives me a momentary look and returns to staring out the window. The passengers are leaning in the aisle, staring back at me. Feeling a little embarrassed and stupid, I give them a little flick of my wrist as if to say mind your own business.

"We are starting our decent, it is sunny and 101 degrees Fahrenheit. Welcome, to Philadelphia," a garbled voice filled the cabin.

The fasten seat belt sign was flashing. The words, "you have got to be kidding," came to mind.

Our footsteps echoed off the corridor walls of the nearly vacant terminal as we headed to baggage claim. There I would pick up my stuff and soon rid myself of my excess baggage, namely Esther. Well that's what I thought, anyway.

We gathered our belongings and exited through the arrivals doors. "That don't sound right." We went out the incoming doors. "No." We left the frigging building.

Zeke was outside waiting outside to take us all back to the cell.

When we got back to the cell, things had changed. As I remember, there were more bodies here before I left for Israel.

It seemed that a rapture, raptor, rupture, or something like that had taken place. The definition Zeke gave me was that it was "a snatching away."

All I know is I was not invited to the party, so, let's leave it at that.

CHAPTER 12

DEVIL'S & DEMON'S & SCI-FI, OH MY

I t was early December and we were in the midst of restructuring shorelines. The extreme heat gave birth to a major glacier meltdown, changing the demographics of the world. The drought was having an opposite effect on inland lakes and ponds. They were shrinking, some to the point of completely drying up.

Also, the war inside America did not seem to be going well. If things didn't change soon, it would be inevitable, our little sanctuary would be sought out.

At this time, we received a message from "Doomsday John." Israel was now in the control of General Ogden Gehrhardt.

Things had not changed, the adversary still wanted Iyov to come into their fold. Yet, they made no attempt to flush him out. It's as though the man had a protective shield around him. Instead, they took a new tactic.

The enemie's new tactic was to go through Iyov's wife, Salome. They wanted her to explain to her husband, what they were offering him. The enemy was ready to return his ranch to him, plus more acres. They would give him a workforce to replace his children in the daily operations of the ranch. With the drought and heat, that meant shelter for the animals and feeding and watering of the same. The biggest selling point was they had doctors that could cure his disease.

Salome was excited about what she had heard and could not wait to relay the offer to her husband. Her hopes were dashed when Iyov rejected the offer.

Everybody has their breaking point and this was Salome's. She had been through a lot and had lost everything. But the final straw was that she was not going to stand by and watch her husband die.

She gave Iyov an ultimatum. If he entered his prayer room, one more time, to speak to this uncaring God, She, would not be there when he came out.

Two things happened when Iyov entered his prayer room. Salome followed through on her threat and the 5th seal was broken. This seal is the Martyr clause, all those being bullied and willing to die for their belief.

***

It was late August and for the last couple months the enemy had been taking daily flights, out of every major airport, to the middle east. It was as though they were abandoning the war effort. They left behind death, destruction and a few meager scraps for the population to fight over. Reports had it, that this anomaly was going on around the globe.

There was something big going down. You just don't take your ball and go home in the middle of the game.

Well anyway, Zeke and I shared a small office/ bed chamber. With one desk, two cots and no room to move about. Our original leader, Lily, had a room three times the size of ours. And since we, assumed she was involved in the snatching away thing and not coming back anytime in the near future, why not trade cramp for comfort.

Zeke and I sought permission from Father Thomas Riley to take ownership of Lily's quarters. Father Riley had control of the cell during Lily's absence and gave us his blessing.

Oh my God, her room was a horde's paradise. If I needed instruction on being a slob, I wanted Lily as my mentor? Right now, this place made my small room look like a mansion.

Since we couldn't get a bulldozer in here, we will have to clean it old fashion way. It took many hours of cleaning but, we were finally done. The room was huge. We could bring in another desk and cot and still have room to host a small get together.

We were so proud of our accomplishment that I gave Zeke a victory lap around the room on the desk chair. I shoved him towards the desk and he plopped his feet on it.

We heard something drop from beneath the desk. Zeke reached under the desk and pulled out a book. He studied the first entry for about five minutes. He then checked the condition of the cover, the binding and discoloration of the pages.

He looked at me stunned. He said the book is seven to ten years old but, dates the first entry to be a Sumerian cuneiform and very, very old. He needed some time to get an accurate translation.

He took Lily's room and I went back to my cubicle. What the hell, I've been there this long another few days won't hurt nothing.

***

Zeke calls me into Lily's room. He is very distraught, yet excited, the book appears to be a parole log. The author is allowed freewill but, must record their actions, the first author was a man named Noach, English translation Noah.

Zeke dated the first entry between 2350 to 2300 BCE. The Akkadians are in control of the land, under the rule of Sargon. It is at this point that God holds three fallen Angels responsible for his upcoming wrath against humanity. The Angels being held accountable are Lilith, the Angel of lust, Djinn, the Angel of desires, and Osiris the reaper, the Angel of death.

Noah was ordered to build a large ocean vessel. He was also ordered to collect blood samples from each kind of animal for re-animation at the appropriate time. They were to be placed on the top two decks in vials.

The three fallen angels, had their spirits encased in vials and placed in the bowels of the ship, to be imprisoned till the final judgement.

Zeke estimated that the actual event took place between 2240 and 2230 BCE. The flood gates were open on the world. His estimation came because of the mention of Sargon's grandson, Naramsin.

The next entry had the vessel grounded somewhere in the mountains of Turkey. Noah is drunk, naked and making a fool of himself. While his sons were tending to him, Curiosity got the better of, Ham's wife, and she snuck into the ship's bowels. Ham was Noah's eldest son. There she somehow released the wayward spirits opening up a Pandora's box.

Authorship and location now shift to Egypt between 1447 and 1445 BCE. There are ten plagues that come upon the land and Pharaoh Amenhotep II. The last of which, gives Osiris open season to take the first born of every family, friend or foe, whose doors are not laced with the blood of a lamb. And ends with a mass migration of a Nomadic people.

Then comes a line of ancestry which leads to a chosen one, yet to make an appearance.

4 BCE during the reign of Herod, the Great. The chosen one has arrived. Osiris' failure to dispose of him angers Satan and from here, the master pulls out all the stops.

29 BCE, Lilith attends the crucifixion of the Christ. Their eyes met briefly and for the first time, Lilith felt the emotion called fear. She saw him look to the heavens and mouth the words, Father forgive them, they no not what they do.

The moment a soldier's spear pierced Christ's side, confirming death, that was sacrifice enough for Satan to open the door where time does not exist. Barabbas, in human form, and Djinn, in spirit, passed through.

October 31, 2022: The portal where time does not exist is again opened. This time without the needed sacrifice due Satan. Osiris and I passed through in the bodies we had possessed on the other side. The co-ordinance put us in the middle of a place called Delaware Bay. We are fished out by Djinn. He had taken the body of a faithless priest by the name of Alexander Gray. Gray's only desire was to be left alone. He got his wish and now resides by himself in the land of nowhere.

With the aid of our allies at BarTech, Osiris and I received our new identities. I was now Lily Faraday and given a high security job at the Pentagon. Djinn was now Saul Linetti and his job, was to track down and make good on the sacrifice due Satan for opening the portal.

Osiris, thumbed through a magazine and took a fancy to the wardrobe of the day. That was enough to start the age - old tension between Osiris and Djinn, when Djinn commented, something about, clothes changing what Osiris was. Lilith had to keep them separated and reminded them of the mission.

March 29, 2023: Barabbas elected Pope.

April 1, 2025: Carl Parkes paid me a visit. He cannot go through with the assignment. His fear of incarceration is just to great. He is a spineless excuse for a human and he must be taken care of. I tell him he is off the hook.

When he leaves, I carefully remove one of his cigarette butts from the ash tray and place it under a lamp post across the street.

April 2, 2025: Detective Braxton pays me a visit. He is a gung- ho cop, that I get the feeling, would shoot first and ask questions later. The perfect patsy to tie up loose ends.

That sort of pissed me off, to think I had been manipulated from day 1.

December 5, 2025: Failure to win over Iyov causes Satan to put his fail- safe plan into action.

"And that, dear Joel, is where it stops," said Zeke.

I lean back, I'm tired. I'm tired of explaining the unexplainable. I'm tired of making excuses for reality. I don't even know what is real, anymore. But I am no quitter and I don't intend to start now.

This seemed like a situation, where the less known by others, the less chance of causing panic. I needed to go directly to "Doomsday John," myself. The last time I pulled a stunt like this, it did not work out so well. I did not want to drag Zeke into it without his permission.

"I have to break protocol, and go right to the top," I informed Zeke.

"We have a protocol," asked Zeke with a smile? "And, what's this I, shouldn't it be we?" he added.

I knew, I liked this guy from the start.

We reached the control room and the door was locked.

"Do you have a key," I asked?

"You're the cop, pick the lock, dumbass," Zeke replied with a grin.

I reached in my wallet and pulled out a credit card. I slid it between the door jam and the latch. With a slight push, we were in. Damn, I thought, credit cards open doors, after all. I closed the door behind us and switched on the light.

"Did you just call me a dumbass," I asked with a smile? Then added, rhetorically," it felt good getting the stress from the inside... outside, huh?

You have got to love the information highway. John had no idea there was any movement of cells on the eastern seaboard. He had, however, suspected there was a breach in the Chapter known as Thyatira, which incidentally was the Chapter of my indoctrination, and what we relayed to him, sort of, confirmed it.

John believed we were being herded together for a mass extinction. Our top priority was to get Esther St. Croix out of there. He gave us the ID and password of the main computer, only Privy to the first and second in command. There we would receive instructions. We were to run a copy and then delete it.

We received the address of a cell in Evansville, Indiana. It belonged to the Chapter of Sardis. From there we would receive further instruction.

We have no choice we have to tell Father Riley. He was not happy that we went over his head. But it wasn't important now. He tossed us the keys to his van, told us to load up supplies and get Esther out of there. He would handle bug out procedures.

"Do you know where you are going," asked Father Riley?

"Yes but, we feel the fewer people that know, the better chance we have," I replied.

"I understand," said Father Riley, "Get Esther out of here."

Zeke, Solomon and I loaded supplies in the van while Jael fetched Esther.

CHAPTER 13

DARKNESS: A HOME FOR THE BLIND

As we drove, the devastation and destruction of the war was evident all around us. We passed by miles and miles of boarded up buildings and homes. Barns collapsing from lack of care. Cities were now virtual Ghost towns. Every once in a while, we would come upon an abandon vehicle or animal carcass along the road.

The longer we drove, the more hopeless things seemed to be. My nerves were taking a beating to the point of making me somewhat short tempered. It did not help that Jael and Zeke were laughing and joking in the back seat, apparently oblivious to our situation. Esther just sat there staring out the window. Every so often she would blurt out a phrase in French. Jael would give her a brief answer, then Esther returned to staring out of the window.

"Hit the gas," said Solomon.

"What's the matter," I asked?

"I'm not sure," he replied. "Just do it."

After about 30 miles I let off the accelerator and asked, "What was that all about?"

Solomon believed we were being followed. At first, he thought they were marauders, a lawless breed in, what has become, a lawless land. The bastards laid siege to anything and attacked anyone to get their daily needs, met. He dismissed that idea because, if they were marauders, they would have attacked already. But it didn't matter anymore, we seem to have lost them.

After a few miles, Solomon said, "They're back."

I had seen or heard nothing but, I trusted Solomon's instinct. With the failure to lose our tail, we have a problem. We have something or someone they are after. Solomon and I both looked back at Esther.

Since they seem to know where we are going, that could only mean one thing, we had an informant in our, midst. The only other person that new our destination was Zeke. But he was almost like a brother to me. I could not and would not believe he would betray us. The facts, though, spoke for themselves. I was breaking a code: Never become personally involved. How could I not? He was a close friend of mine. Still, a dark cloud, of doubt, hovered over him and I felt ashamed just thinking it.

The other scenario was that someone in Evansville was not who they claimed to be. Just to ease my mind, I chose to believe that option.

We finally made it to our destination. Lying outside, on what use to be a lawn, were the nude bodies of three females. Upon closer inspection, they were beaten, bruised and apparently molested. We would get no answers from two of them, they were dead. The third did not look in any shape to talk to anyone.

Zeke went to get a shovel for burial purposes while Jael tended to the lone surviving female. Solomon and I headed to the boarded-up farmhouse. It was closed up to detour any curiosity seekers from believing there was anything of value inside. I guess it didn't work to well.

As we climbed the porch stairs, we heard a groan. A male, badly beaten, with a bloody 2 x 4 lying next to him was our groaner. We helped him onto the porch swing.

"By the looks of the blood on that wood, they did a pretty good number on you," I said.

"Hell, that, ain't my blood," he replied. "I put a pretty good hurt on a couple of them before they got me." Suddenly, there was a concern in his tone, "The girls, where are the girls?"

"I'm sorry, but, two of them are gone," Solomon said.

"Shit, shit, shit," said the man. "Which two?"

"A heavyset white woman," Solomon answered.

"Diane," said the man painfully.

"And a young African American."

"Tisha," he replied, shaking his head.

The man's name was Jonah Stucky, he was the head of this cell. He claimed it was marauders that were responsible for the death of the women. The bandits were in the process of taking anything of value to them, when they heard us coming and fled.

It sounded a little too convenient. Outside of a bump on his head, which could have been a birth defect, and a little blood on his lip, there was just a small sign of a struggle. And that could be from the girls protecting themselves. "Are you sure the blood on that wood doesn't belong to those women," I inquired sarcastically? Sure, it was a stretch but, I was grasping at straws to exonerate Zeke of any wrong doing.

"Hell no," screamed Jonah! "And I don't think I like your tone. I certainly don't care for your accusation."

"Look, I'm not going to apologize for my attitude," I said." But, we have a mole amongst us and I'm not crazy about rats."

Jonah appeared to be reaching for the bloody 2x4, perhaps to pummel me with it.

Damn, he was pissed.

"Maybe you're the rat tough guy," said Jonah.

"You made a mistake," I started. "You left a witness."

"Whoa, whoa, whoa, both of you," Solomon said stepping in. "Let's not play the blame game without concrete evidence."

Solomon asked Jonah if there were any instructions for us and where they were? Solomon then told me to go retrieve them. I think, just to keep Jonah and I separated.

"While, you're in there, grab my smokes and flask from the drawer, tough guy" Jonah yelled to me as I entered the house.

"Damn right I'm a tough guy," I said pulling my weapon from my belt and waving it in the air. "And I have the gun to prove it."

"If you feel up to it, Jonah? Solomon said. "I would like to get a little background on the surviving young lady."

Her name was Rhonda Jericho. They had dubbed her "Rehab" as a pet name. It seems her boyfriend had cleaned out their bank account and took off. She had been a prostitute/drug addict in Indianapolis, servicing both friend and foe. With the exodus of the enemy, our soldiers going home and the general depletion of humanity, there were not enough resources to keep her addiction satisfied. She headed south hoping to find greener pastures. Her car had broken down about a mile from the Farm. She was found wandering outside, in a confused state, by Diane. She had been with them ever since.

Rehabilitation of Rhonda had been slow. There were no drugs, other than Jonah's whiskey, on the premises. She had to quit cold turkey and that was not a pleasant scene. Her moods went from fear and delusion to violent outbursts. As time went by, the episodes were diminishing in length and frequency. She was not quite where they wanted her to be but, she was progressing. She did not need what happened today. But it happened, nothing can be done about that.

Meanwhile, I was rummaging through papers on the desk. Too bad I was not here to teach them my filing system. Ah ha, Found it. The message was a simple code and read: Santa Anna for the last supper Alamode.

OK, I can do this, think. Santa Anna, Santa Anna, What, does that mean? Santa Ana, California is most likely underwater. The spelling, that's it. If you had watched as many westerns as I did as a kid, Santa Anna was not a place, but a person. He was the Mexican

General that led the assault on the Alamo. Now, Last Supper Alamode. What a strange combination of words. The more I stared, the more I focused on Alamode. Suddenly, Alamo just jumped out at me. Seems our next stop would be San Antonio, Texas.

I reached into the desk and pulled out Jonah's cigarettes and flask. I looked around to make sure no one was watching. I opened the flask and took a hit. It was just to settle my nerves. At least, that was as good excuse as any.

I went out to the porch, showed Solomon the message and gave him my interpretation. He concurred with my translation.

"Great," I said. "Let's get outta here."

"Hold on," replied Solomon. "Jonah is not finished praying over the graves."

"They're not coming with us, are they," I inquired?

My excuse was that we were already cramped together in the van and we would need to share our rations with two more people. But the real reason was, I just did not like this Jonah guy. I don't know why? He never did anything to me.

"Of course, they're coming with us," Solomon replied. "We cannot, just, abandon them."

His argument was weak, based on morality and what was right. Words that no longer had a place in this world. In the end Solomon wins, Solomon always wins.

Solomon and I went to meet Zeke by the van as Jael was bringing Rhonda back to join us. Jael was not a big woman by any stretch, yet, the clothing she gave Rhonda to wear hung loosely over her skeletal frame. Her long red hair was wet and plastered against her body. Her cheeks sunken in and eyes that seemed to bulge from her skull. Rhonda did not speak. She did not look at you, she looked through you as though you were not there. And every move she made had to be orchestrated by someone else. She gave me the creeps.

Jonah came over and grabbed Rhonda by the arm. "Come, dear, we're going to take a little ride."

Suddenly, every light source in the heavens had been turned off and darkness was upon the face of the earth.

"We have to move," said Solomon. "The 6th seal has been broken."

"What the hell does that mean!" I exclaimed.

"It means, Jesus Christ has left the building," replied Solomon.

As we headed towards the van, Zeke said, "that was a good one, Solomon."

"Why, thank you Ezekiel, Sometimes I can have a sense of humor."

"I'm glad you two find our situation funny," I said.

We piled in the van Solomon got behind the wheel and started it up.

"Do you have a driver's license," I asked?

"Why, are you with the license bureau?" Solomon answered.

"You're on a roll, Solomon, said Zeke. "You should bring that side of you out more often."

" Ya, he's a belly full of laughs," I said fighting sarcasm with sarcasm

"Look," Solomon started. "All of you come to me for advice and guidance, I'm just as human as the next person. I do not have all the answers."

Well anyway we continued our westward trek. We stopped at the Mississippi river to replenish our water supply. The water was still fresh. There appeared to be enough volume and force to prevent the ocean from backing up this far North.

As we crossed the bridge to Missouri, In the darkness, I noticed a dozen, or so, candle lit homes. We were not alone in this world. It looked as though this was a spot, some of what remained of the population had chosen to recolonize. Dare I even dream that places like Chicago or Cleveland would be prime real estate and far more advanced in they're progression.

We continued our journey in an erratic fashion. We would serpentine 5 miles southwest, 10 miles northwest and then return to our original route. The cycle just repeated itself over and over again. All the excess movement was to try and lose the tail Solomon had claimed was following us.

Now, I had not seen or heard anyone behind us. I was beginning to wonder if there was anyone, really, back there or if Solomon's imagination was playing games with him.

Whatever the case, I was the one paying the price for his paranoia. Since we had to improvise, I had to syphon what remained in every abandon vehicles gas tank, we passed, to replenish our supply.

I swallowed so much gas that if I were to fart I would have blown us all to kingdom come.

84

CHAPTER 14

NO VACANCY AT THE TOP

San Antonio was just another American ghost town, void of life. We pulled up to the main entrance of the, once beautiful structure called the Alamo and proceeded to dig out all of our candles, lanterns and flashlights. We set up shop near the main entrance.

Our next job was to try and locate our instructions. This was going to be like looking for a needle in a haystack. Each of us took a flashlight and separated. I happened to look back and Solomon had not moved. He stood there staring at a painting on the wall.

"Are you going to help," I asked?

He just nodded at the picture on the wall.

"It's the last supper; oh, the last supper," I said, finally catching on.

Solomon took the painting down as I gathered everyone together. He tore the backing paper off and there was an envelope within. Inside the envelope was a map and a letter. He opened the letter and began to read:

Esther's daughter is alive and well. She was found crying in a dumpster

by a homeless woman. The baby was brought to the church. For the

child's safety, I had her sent to Santa Fe, New Mexico. She was put

in the foster care of Mary and Joseph Hope.

Now, to business, For, too long the Holy one has taken a backseat to

Religion. And God will not tolerate, that. Your assignment is to get

Esther here, to join her daughter and myself. Together, we shall rebuild

The Church. It will not be a building yet, the foundation will be built

Of worship for the one and only merciful God.

From this day forward, Esther shall be known as Destiny And her

Daughter shall be called Grace.

God is with you!

Signed,

Bishop Angelo De Leone

AKA

Peter, Guardian Angel of the Church

A crystal clear, clarity and calming peace came over my entire being. It was like nothing I have ever experienced. Human words could not do justice to my feeling, so I will make no attempt to express them.

I did know that, my whole life, I had been living a lie. I viewed God in the same context with, and pertaining to, Religion. I now realize, the two are as different as day and night. God is not the architect of a terrorist plot, Religion is. The problem with Religion is it tries to shape and manipulate God to fit in they're belief system. You don't fix God, God fixes you.

This feeling I had was much bigger than I was and I wanted to hold onto it a bit longer. Alone in the darkness outside seemed like the appropriate place to delve deeper into, what was for me, unprecedented territory. Maybe God would meet me in the porch area and we could discuss all the secrets and mystic that make God, God. I was a little disappointed when this Holy Entity was not there. But perhaps somethings are not meant to be known.

I thought of my mom, oh, how I missed her so. But I now began to realize what she was all about. She was the difference between, the favor of God and being chosen by God. To be favored is to receive earthly rewards and to be chosen is to receive bigger rewards in the afterlife. Many are favored, few are chosen, because, few can handle the responsibility that comes from being chosen. My mom, in no way, shape or form was ever favored by God. I do, however, believe she was among the chosen. That put her in the company of the elite. There was Mother Terasa. She started with the favor of God then had to relinquish all worldly possessions to become one of the Elite. And then there was Moses. He led a multitude of grumbling people though the dessert, for 40 years, in search of the promised land. When arriving at the border of the land flowing with milk and honey, Everyone, was allowed entrance except Moses.

And the revelations just kept coming as Destiny came to mind. Until recently, she had never, even, heard of San Antonio. Then there was myself, if I had a list of 100 places I would like to be, San Antonio would not be on it yet, here we both were. It took God many years, many road blocks and an army of people to get me here. Exactly, where I'm Suppose, to be.

The extreme heat and drought came to mind. Possibly there was nothing scientific about it. If we choose to worship false idols, we can have them. See if they can get us a cool day or an afternoon shower.

Zeke and destiny rushed past me, disturbing my journey into the land of make believe and I returned to my regular charming self. Zeke started the van and I saw a faint red flashing, in the darkness, under the wheel well.

I walked to the van and told Zeke not to turn off the engine and not put it in gear. I went to the hatch and pulled out a tire iron, crawled under the fender and pried the mechanism off. It stopped blinking. Damn, it was a tracking device.

I was pissed and human nature took charge. I slammed the device to the ground, stomped on it and beat the hell out of it and cursed at it, like it understood me, till all that was left was broken plastic and shredded wire.

I dropped to my knees, threw my arms to the heavens and cried," What do you want from me?"

I returned to my senses after my little temper tantrum. What I had just done, had caused irreversible damage. I could have attached the device to another vehicle and sent our tail in a different direction. But now, that was no longer an alternative and it would not be long before the enemy realizes something is wrong.

More composed, I again looked to the heavens. "God you have my attention, let's talk."

I remember the signature on the letter that was just read. Father Thomas Riley was the only one that led me to believe Bishop Angelo de Leone was dead. The most Damning evidence, though, was Riley freely gave us the keys to his van. We had our mole.

Now, why a tracking device and not a bomb? A bomb could have eliminated Destiny and the rest of us would have been a bonus.

The only reasonable answer was they knew Destiny's child, Grace, still lives and Destiny was the bait leading them to her.

I knew what I had to do. I didn't much like the answer but, it was what it was. I walked to the window of the van.

"Are you coming," Zeke asked?

"No, I have a job to do and it ends right here," I replied.

Zeke and Destiny drove off as I headed back to the building. As much as I believed myself to be a super cop, I was not. So, what form of madness has come upon me?

I entered the building and Rhonda was sitting a few feet away from the door. She was uttering or chanting or I don't know what you would call it? But she was making sounds like thunder and lightning, a babbling brook and a breeze rustling through the trees.

Not the sounds you write or describe in conversation but, the literal sounds these entities make. Rhonda never failed in her attempts to give me the heebie jeebies.

In another corner of the room, Jonah was digging out rifles and ammo. He handed them to Solomon and Jael. They in turn loaded the weapons.

Suddenly, there was the roar of engines and headlights flooded the room. Then silence and darkness returned.

"Hey, tough guy, do you want a rifle or would you rather go out there and arrest them," Jonah asked me?

Something told me to apologize to Jonah for being such a shit to him. So, I did. The only other person I had ever apologized to was, Delilah, my wife and that was, always, just to get her off my back.

Solomon gathered everyone for his prayer session. This time I joined in and became a participant. With death looming outside of these walls, I was grasping onto this God like a baby clinging to its mother.

Solomon never ended his prayers with a simple "Amen" but with "Let It Be So," as if it were a command, not a request.

We broke the circle and I noticed the door was ajar. Rhonda was no longer at the table. All that remained was a candle, a bloody right thumb and a pair of garden shears. I started after her and Solomon grabbed my arm and shook his head. I drew my pistol and took a position by a window. I don't know why? I could not see clearly in the darkness.

Jonah took up a spot near me and offered me a hit from his flask. I took it.

Jael and Solomon engaged in a long embrace and prolonged kiss before assuming their positions.

'WHO THE HELL IS THIS," a male voice boomed?

"I AM JUSTICE AND I HAVE COME FOR YOU," Rhonda replied in a tone just as loud.

The next thig I heard was a pop from a gun and saw the flash. As Rhonda's body hit the ground the whole area lit up. In the sky were, what appeared to be, Bio – Illuminated beings on horseback. Everywhere they had been, the light remained.

I could now focus on the adversary. Standing over Rhonda, gun barrel still smoking, was a man dressed to the nines, fedora and all. It was the same man who stood on my front lawn the night of my wife's death. I made an educated assumption that it was this guy Linetti, I heard mention of.

Behind him, I guessed, were about 20 soldiers. There were also, 5 jeeps with gun turrets mounted on the back. They also had an anti – armor tank, probably why they moved so slow and a little bit of an overkill. To top it all off, they had a large supply truck.

My evaluation was bleak. We were out - numbered, they had superior firepower and enough supplies to wait us out.

"Send out Esther St Croix and the rest of you are free to walk," yelled Saul Linetti.

"We know no one by that name," replied Solomon. "And even if we did, why would we turn her over to you?"

"Because, it seems, you are out of options," came the reply.

"Give us 15 minutes to discuss it," said Solomon.

"You have 5 minutes," answered Linetti.

I whispered to Solomon, "Do you know what you're doing?"

Solomon just smiled.

Oh no, I thought, this had all the signs of not ending well.

"Your time is up," yelled Linetti.

"No, your time is up, Osiris," replied Solomon.

A barrage of gunfire broke out from both sides. Every missile that hit our fortress took away a little more of our protective wall. The last thing I remember was a bullet passing through my left shoulder.

EPILOGUE

HAPPILY, EVER AFTER

I neatly fold the papers, put them back in briefcase, and sit back to ponder my situation. I have a can of beans and a half a canteen of water. It is more than obvious that I must move on.

Perhaps I'll backtrack to St Louis and eventually head North to the Great Lakes area. It is a good plan, except it is flawed. I have no compass and with no sun or distinguishable landmark, my sense of direction does not exist.

"Ok God, you're up, lead away."

As I wait for the neon lights and flashing arrows pointing this way, stupid, I begin to whistle. "That's a catchy tune. What is it called? Why am I talking to myself?" I start to whistle again. "Damn, I stink, I need a shower." I return to whistling. "Ok God, That's it!! When you needed me, you would not shut up, Now, I need you and all I get is the silent treatment."

I hear trumpets and singing getting louder the closer it gets. I turn and see a multitude of, what appears to be, illuminated humanoid beings. It was hard to tell. It was like looking at a light bulb glowing in the daylight. You could see it was on but it did not emit the radiance.

The crowd came to a halt along with the music and singing. One of the beings approaches me. I scour the ground for something I can use as a weapon, to no avail. The entity stops a few feet away from me.

"Who are you," I ask?

This being brings his pointer finger to his lips and makes a shh sound. "Relax Joel, it is all over. The 7th seal has been broken."

The 7th seal was the actual eviction. Satan and his followers were exiled to the lake of Sulphur.

I have no clue as to what is going on here. I search the crowd seeking some kind of satisfactory answer. And there she was, right up front, same smile I remember as a child and no artificial aid to assist her in movement.

"Momma," I say as I go towards her.

The being raises his hand and it was like I hit a glass barrier. All my forward progress came to a halt. "I'm sorry Joel, that's as close as I can allow you to get."

I continue to scan the beings. "Where's my dad?"

His prolonged silence was all the answer I required.

An unthinkable scenario suddenly hit me and I have to ask. "Am I dead?"

"No, you're alive along with 144,000 of your kind," comes the reply.

Mom had always told me that the meek would inherit the earth. In no way did I fit that category, leaving me more confused about what was going on.

"I have some cash, can I buy some food and drink from you," I ask?

"I'm sorry, Joel, we have no need of such things," comes the reply.

"If I am not dead and cannot join you, can I inquire, what business you have with me," I ask?

"I have no business with you," he replies. "We are seeking out a spot for the next Garden of Eden, where God can place the new creation."

"Whaaaat?" I say, very much confused.

"Oh yes, it has been done many times before and the Holy One will continue to do it till humanity gets it right," says the being.

I had read the first three chapters of the bible. If evil has been vanquished, there is no temptation, therefore, no original sin. The human race has to get it right this time. I bring this to his attention.

"Yes," he replies. "But Satan and Lilith had a baby and the Almighty can refuse no child access to the kingdom."

The beings begin to fade, "wait, I have more," they disappear, "questions?"

I feel a sharp pain in my left shoulder and my eyes spring open. I am encased in a tomb of rock and the weight of my confinement restricts movement. Light penetrates through a small slit before my eyes and I can see the barren landscape outside of my prison.

A large locust lands on the crack and stares me down. Behind it, the ground is covered with a horde of those nasty vermin.

The tune I was whistling earlier clicks in my head. I sing, "Jesus loves me this I know, for the bible tells me so."

The locust flutters from the crack. I see the dust kick up as the rest of those abominations form a large black cloud and follow the leader, away from me, till they vanish from my sight.

I gaze into the vast expanse of the abyss. I feel the presence of Osiris but I fear him not. As my body slips into eternal slumber, I listen to the creaking of a rocking chair on a hardwood floor.

.

T..........H..........E

E

N

D